Drawing MONSTERS Step-by-Step

Drawing GHOSTS

Carter Hayn

WINDMILL BOOKS

New York

Published in 2013 by Windmill Books, LLC

Copyright © 2013 by Windmill Books, LLC

CREDITS:
Book Design: Nathalie Beullens-Maoui
Art by Planman, Ltd.

Photo Credits: Cover, p. 20 Image by Catherine MacBride/Flickr/Getty Images; p. 4 Christophe Testi/Shutterstock.com (pencil); p. 5 Obak/Shutterstock.com (paper), Paul Matthew Photography/Shutterstock.com (eraser), 2happy/Shutterstock.com (marker), Iv Nikolny/Shutterstock.com (pencils); p. 6 SuperStock/Getty Images; p. 8 The Bridgeman Art Library/Getty Images; p. 10 Hulton Archive/Getty Images; p. 12 Archive Photos/Moviepix/Getty Images; p. 14 Ghislain & Marie David de Lossy/Cultura/Getty Images; p. 16 M. Eric Honeycutt/Vetta/Getty Images; p. 18 H. Armstrong Roberts/Retrofile/Getty Images.

Cataloging-in-Publication Data

Hayn, Carter.
Drawing Ghosts / by Carter Hayn.
    p. cm. — (Drawing monsters step-by-step)
Includes index.
ISBN 978-1-61533-690-6 (library binding) — ISBN 978-1-61533-700-2 (pbk.) — ISBN 978-1-61533-701-9 (6-Pack)
1. Ghosts in art — Juvenile literature. 2. Monsters in art — Juvenile literature. 3. Drawing — Technique — Juvenile literature. I. Title.
NC825.M6 H39 2013
743.8'7—dc23

Manufactured in the United States of America

For more great fiction and nonfiction, go to www.windmillbooks.com.

CPSIA Compliance Information: Batch #BW13WM: For further information contact Windmill Books, New York, New York at 1-866-478-0556.

Ghosts or Spirits	4
Do Not Disturb!	6
Restless Spirits	8
Ghostly Revenge	10
Ghosts with a Message	12
Hauntings	14
Ghostly Apparitions	16
Trick or Treat!	18
Ghosts in Science	20
Monster Fun Facts	22
Glossary	23
Read More	23
Index	24
Websites	24

Ghost stories have existed since the time of the ancient Egyptians. There were tales of ghosts throughout the Greek and Roman eras, Medieval times, and the present day. Ghosts represent people's fears of the unknown and the afterlife.

In stories and legends, ghosts are believed to be the spirits of dead people or animals that are seen or heard by the living. Ghosts may be described as invisible or barely visible, and sometimes they appear lifelike. Many movies, stories, and books have been written about ghosts. In this book you will read about and draw several kinds of these scary spirits.

YOU WILL NEED THE FOLLOWING SUPPLIES:

PAPER

PENCIL

ERASER

RULER

COLORED PENCILS

MARKER

Do Not Disturb!

Some religions believe that **disturbing** ghosts will bring curses to those who call them. In the Bible for instance, it is told that King Saul of Israel asked a **medium** to call up the soul of the **prophet** Samuel.

The ghost of Samuel appears. He is not happy at being disturbed, and he angrily tells King Saul that he has disobeyed God and predicts Saul's tragic end.

The next day Saul's army was defeated in battle, and he died soon after.

Samuel's ghost shocked and frightened Saul.

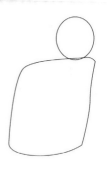

STEP 1

Draw the outline of the body. Add a circle for the head.

STEP 2

Add small circles and ovals around the body.

STEP 3

Add the outline of the sheet, over the head and the shoulders.

STEP 4

Draw the hands, arms, and the folds of the sheet.

STEP 5

Add details to the sheet. Draw clouds in the background.

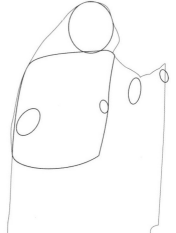

STEP 6

Erase the guides. Draw the folds in the sheet and add details. Color your drawing.

Restless Spirits

Native Americans also have legends about ghosts, or spirits. As in many other **cultures**, these spirits can be good or evil, yet they all have one thing in common. They are all believed to be souls of the dead who are not at peace.

Some Native American legends say that when someone was not buried properly, or if their grave was disturbed, their spirit could not rest. A restless spirit was said to then be doomed to roam the earth.

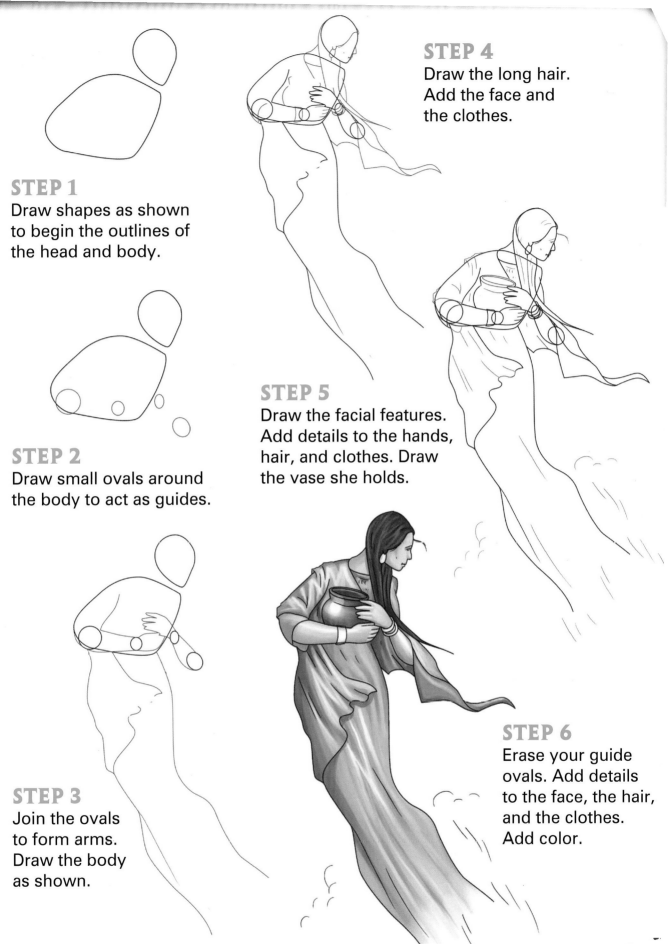

STEP 1

Draw shapes as shown to begin the outlines of the head and body.

STEP 2

Draw small ovals around the body to act as guides.

STEP 3

Join the ovals to form arms. Draw the body as shown.

STEP 4

Draw the long hair. Add the face and the clothes.

STEP 5

Draw the facial features. Add details to the hands, hair, and clothes. Draw the vase she holds.

STEP 6

Erase your guide ovals. Add details to the face, the hair, and the clothes. Add color.

Ghostly Revenge

Many books have been written in which one of the characters is a ghost. The ghosts are sometimes evil, and sometimes they are good and helpful. Others are simply looking for **revenge**.

In William Shakespeare's play *Hamlet*, Hamlet's father came back as a ghost to tell Hamlet that he had been murdered. He wanted his son to revenge for his death.

Hamlet has doubts that what the ghostsays is true. Once he discovers the truth, Hamlet decides to kill his father's murderer. However, many lives are lost in the process.

STEP 1
Draw a round shape for the head and a larger shape for the body.

STEP 4
Draw the beard, eyebrows, and nose. Add the outline of the ghost's clothing.

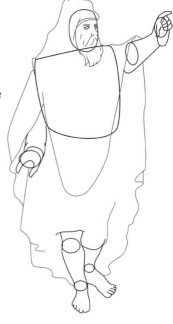

STEP 2
Draw small circles and ovals around the body.

STEP 5
Add details to the face, the clothes, and the top of the head.

STEP 3
Use the circles and ovals to guide you in drawing the arms, legs, hands, and feet. Add rounded shapes for the eyes.

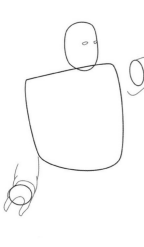

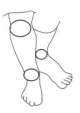

STEP 6
Erase the guide shapes. Add more details to the clothing and color your drawing.

Ghosts with a Message

A well-known story about ghosts is *A Christmas Carol* by Charles Dickens. In this story, Ebenezer Scrooge is first visited by the ghost of his friend Jacob Marley, who warns him against his greed.

Scrooge is then visited by three more ghosts. The Ghost of Christmas Past, the Ghost of Christmas Present, and the Ghost of Christmas Yet to Come, appear one by one. They show Scrooge how his behavior has hurt others, and what will happen if he does not change. Because of these ghostly visits, Scrooge realizes that he's been wrong, and he changes his ways.

A Christmas Carol was published in 1843. This is the ghost of Jacob Marley in the 1938 movie version.

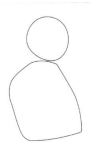

STEP 1

Draw the head, and draw the outline of the body.

STEP 2

Draw two ovals as shown. These will help you draw the arms.

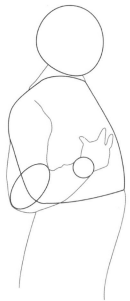

STEP 3

Join the round shapes to form arm and hand. Add lines for the neck and the legs.

STEP 4

Draw the outline of the face, the eyes, eyebrows, hair, nose, and mouth. Draw the outlines of the clothing and the weights.

STEP 5

Draw the outline of the chains. Add the other details to the clothing, face, and hair.

STEP 6

Erase the guides. Add the final details. Color your drawing.

Hauntings

Popular culture tells of ghosts and haunted houses. Haunted houses are sais to be **inhabited** by spirits wthat used to live in the house, or that were familiar with the house.

A haunted house, usually, is said to have cold spots, creaking sounds, and other strange noises. Some people report doors closing suddenly, objects falling, and feeling a "presence." Most of the houses people claim to be haunted are old, drafty houses. The noises and cold spots probably come from the structure of the house or do they?

The most-haunted house in the US is said to be the Whaley House in San Diego, CA.

STEP 1
Draw a shape for the outline of the ghost.

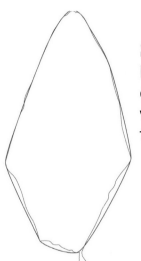

STEP 2
Draw a more detailed shape with wrinkles in the cloth.

STEP 3
Add the pleats to the bottom of the cloth.

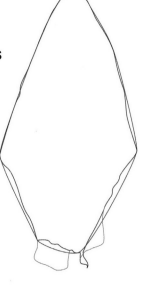

STEP 4
Add a second pleat to the bottom of the cloth.

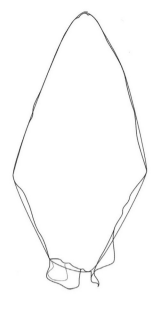

STEP 5
Draw the folds in the cloth.

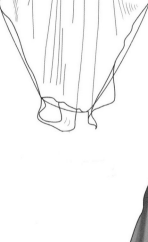

STEP 6
Erase extra lines. Add more details to the cloth and color your drawing.

Ghostly Apparitions

Throughout history there have been many stories about haunted houses. During Roman times, a statesman wrote about a haunted villa in Athens, Greece. It was then discovered that a man had been buried in the yard of the house!

People who have spent the night at 50 Berkeley Square have later become mentally ill. This has been blamed on the house's ghost.

In the 1900s, 50 Berkeley Square became known as the most haunted house in London, England. It is said to have had several **apparitions**, or ghosts that appear before the living. The most common one is of a young woman.

STEP 1
Begin your drawing with two shapes, an oval for the head, and one for the body as shown.

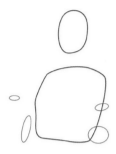

STEP 2
Draw circles to serve as guides for the arms.

STEP 3
Join the circles to form the arms and hands. Draw the outline of the dress. Add lines for the neck.

STEP 4
Draw the headpiece and add details to the dress. Draw the outline of the hair.

STEP 5
Add details to the face, hands, and dress.

STEP 6
Erase extra lines. Add more details to the face, dress, and headpiece. Color your drawing.

Trick or Treat!

Did you know that there is a holiday that celebrates ghosts and spirits? Many people dress up as ghosts on October 31 to celebrate Halloween, or All Hallow's Eve. Dressing up as a ghost is easy. A sheet with two holes for eyes makes for a simple, scary costume.

The tradition of going door-to-door on Halloween dates back to the Middle Ages. It is believed to have started in Ireland and England. In both places, poor people would go door-to-door offering prayers for the dead in exchange for food. The prayers were for a holiday called All Saint's Day, which is November 1.

All Hallow's Eve, or Halloween, is the night before All Hallow's Day, or All Saint's Day. Traditionally, celebration of All Saint's Day began at sundown Halloween.

STEP 1
Draw the two shapes
as shown.

STEP 2
Draw an outline of the sheet
draping over the ghost.

STEP 3
Add two shapes on the
head for the eye holes.

STEP 4
Draw details on the
sheet to show the
folds in the cloth.

STEP 5
Add details on
the sheet.

STEP 6
Erase the guide lines.
Draw some more
folds on the sheet.
Color your drawing.

Ghosts in Science

Some scientists believe that ghosts can be explained away as **optical illusions** or **hallucinations**. For example, a light from a passing car that is reflected through a window could be seen like a ghost. Other scientists think that when we are tired, our minds can play tricks on us.

What is true is that ghost stories have been around throughout human history. Whether they are real or not, the fact is that they exist in many cultures, and they continue to fascinate people to this day.

Many ghosts are said to roam the streets and cemetery of New Orleans, but the most famous one is the ghost of Marie Laveau, the Voodoo Queen of New Orleans!

STEP 1

Draw the outline of
the head and the body
as shown.

STEP 2

Draw two circles as
guides for the hands.

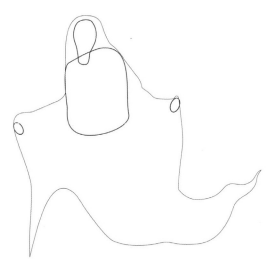

STEP 3

Using the guide shapes,
draw the cloth that is
draped over the body.

STEP 4

Add details to the
cloth. Draw folds
on the front.
Draw the hands.

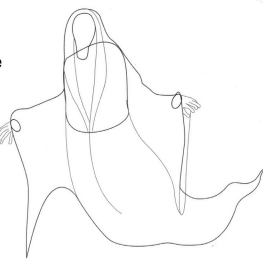

STEP 5

Draw detailed folds.
Add the facial features
and claws.

STEP 6

Erase the guide lines. Add
finishing details and color.

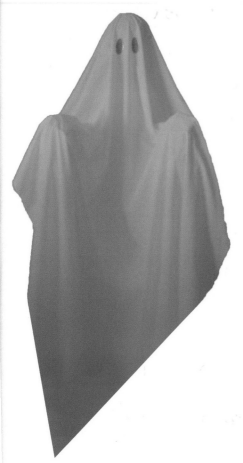

- Some scientists have found that very low sounds, which humans can not consciously hear, can casue a sense of fear and even blurred vision. Scientists think that this might explain the feeling of a place being haunted.

- **Ectoplasm**, a gas like substance supposedly made by ghosts, might actually be will-o'-the-wisp. Will-o'-the-wisp is a light created by decomposing matter. In old cemeteries, the light could be seen hovering over the tombs. This made people believe that it was spirits rising out of their grave.

- Some people say that the White House is haunted. The ghost of first lady Abigail Adams, the wife of John Adams, is said to roam its halls. And Abraham Lincoln is said to have appeared in the Lincoln Bedroom.

- Some people believe that animals can be ghosts, too. The Gettysburg Battefield is said to have ghosts not only of dead Civil War soldiers, but of their horses.

Glossary

APPARITIONS (ap-uh-RIH-shunz) Ghosts.

CULTURES (KUL-churz) The beliefs, practices, and arts of groups of people.

DISTURBING (dih-STERB-ing) Bothering something.

ECTOPLASM (EK-toh-plah-zum) The gaslike light said to be given off by ghosts.

HALLUCINATIONS (huh-LOO-sin-ay-shunz) Things that someone sees that are not really there.

INHABITED (in-HA-but-ed) Lived in a certain place.

LEGENDS (LEH-jends) Stories, passed down through the years, that cannot be proved.

MEDIUM (MEE-dee-umz) People who claim to have contact with the spirit world.

OPTICAL ILLUSIONS (OP-tih-kul ih-LOO-zhunz) Something that tricks the eyes.

PROPHET (PRAH-fet) Someone who says he or she brings messages from God.

REVENGE (rih-VENJ) Hurting someone in return for hurting you.

Bridges, Shirin Yim. *Horrible Hauntings: An Augmented Reality Collection of Ghosts and Ghouls*. Foster City, CA: Goosebottom Books, 2012.

Simon, Seymour. *Ghosts*. Mineola, NY: Dover Children's Books, 2012.

Tallerico, Tony. *Monsters: A Step-by-Step Guide for the Aspiring Monster-Maker*. Mineola, NY: Dover Publications, 2010.

A
All Saints' Day, 18
apparitions, 16

C
Christmas Carol, A, 12

D
Dickens, Charles, 12

H
Halloween, 18
haunted houses, 14, 22

N
Native Americans, 8

R
restless spirits, 8
revenge, 10

S
Samuel, 6
Saul, King, 6
scientific explanations, 20
Scrooge, Ebenezer, 12
Shakespeare, William, 10

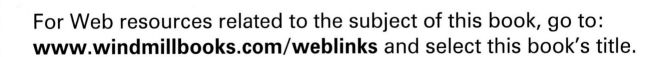

For Web resources related to the subject of this book, go to:
www.windmillbooks.com/weblinks and select this book's title.